MAKE MAGIC! DO GOOD!

First edition 2012

Library of Congress Catalog Card Number 2012942305

ISBN 978-0-7636-5746-8

12 13 14 15 16 17 SCP 10 9 8 7 6 5 4 3 2 1

Printed in Humen, Dongguan, China

This book was typeset in Dante.
The illustrations were done in two parts positive vibes and
three parts watercolor rainbow sprinkles.

Candlewick Press
99 Dover Street
Somerville, Massachusetts 02144

visit us at www.candlewick.com

Dedicated to those
who make good

MAKE MAGIC! DO GOOD!
DALLAS CLAYTON

CANDLEWICK PRESS

THE BOY
WITH
THE
BEARD

The boy with the beard
was the best in his life
when he was six years old.

The fastest, the strongest,
the smartest, the toughest,
so brave, so big, and so bold.

The boy with the beard
was his best at age six
so he decided he wouldn't be seven.
He'd stay six on through eight,
six on through nine,
six on through ten and eleven.

The boy with the beard stayed six
through his teens
on through twenty
and thirty
and years in betweens.

The boy with the beard
stayed six his whole life
with no job
and no house
and no car and no wife.
The boy with the beard had
   no worries at all.
He was six,
he was perfect,
he was having a ball.

Except for one thing
he eventually learned:
that as everyone grew
everyone turned
into something brand-new
while he stayed the same:
a six-year-old boy
with a beard
and a cane.

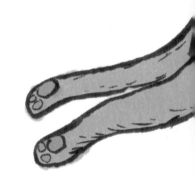

When you're running fast as lightning
it's easy to lose your mind
it's easy to laugh at all the folks
that you're passing and leavin' behind
but you won't be fast forever
so the clever thing to do
is to stop and help the others keep up
because someday
they'll be you.

RUNNING!

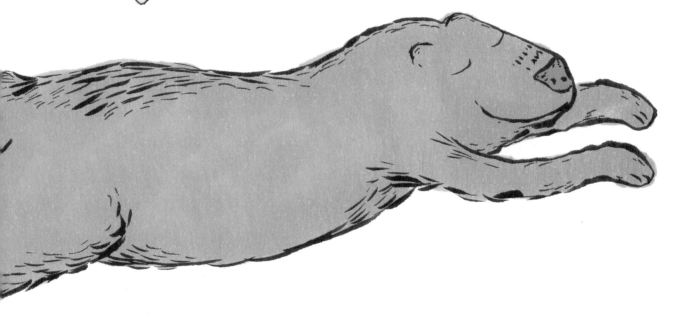

A BLUE APPLE

I ate a blue apple
I shouldn't have done it
but it really looked quite yummy
it's the only blue apple that's ever existed
now it's down inside my tummy.
I don't know if I would do it again
that's a lesson they never teach
but I know one thing's for sure, my friend:
I'd eat a purple peach.

GENIUS

I never worked on rockets
never built a big machine
never counted numbers in my head
to one million billion-teen.

I never was a genius
so I went a different route
and I wrote down all the things
   I figured
every time I figured 'em out.

And I sent 'em to all the geniuses
in hopes that I could help
them figure out a thing or two
they couldn't figure out themselves.

Then maybe they'd get their
   rockets higher
or maybe discover a new
   kind of fire
or maybe they'd smile
or maybe they'd laugh
or maybe they'd go take a
   nice long bath.

And the things I'd figured
would hit 'em just right
and they'd wake up
in the dark of the night
with one small idea
that would change things forever
and make this whole world
just a little bit better.

The effort is the same,
you know,
thinking good
as thinking bad,
saying nice
instead of mean,
making happy,
making sad.
You could
paint up on a building
all the thoughts you ever had
about what's gone wrong
and who's to blame
and what really makes you mad.
Or you could gather up your paints instead
and draw pictures in a pad
and hand them out
to everyone
you ever thought was rad.

THE ARTIST

NEW BEST FRIEND

You're my new best friend
I never met
you're awesome, perfect, swell.
We do everything together
and we get along so well
you're my new best friend I never met
and I love you more than you know
you're my new best friend
I never met
because I never said "Hello."

AMANDA THE PANDA

Amanda the panda
devoured bamboo:
bamboo pancakes, bamboo stew,
bamboo cereal, bamboo pie,
bamboo burgers, bamboo fries,
bamboo syrup on a bamboo cake,
with bamboo sprinkles on her
bamboo shake.

She'd clean her plate and
    empty her cup
then go back for more and
    gobble it up.

But then one day
just after brunch
when she'd eaten bamboo,
a very large bunch,

she looked around
at a truly sad sight
all the bamboo was gone,
every last bite.

The whole bamboo forest,
she'd eaten it bare.
No more bamboo here.
No more bamboo there.
No more bamboo dinner.
No more bamboo lunch.
No more bamboo breakfast.
No more bamboo brunch.
No more bamboo anything
for me or for you
because Amanda the panda
ate too much bamboo.

Did you hear about the race?
Hooray! I came in second place.
And second place will do just fine
in a race to hug a porcupine.

Rundlett Middle School
Concord, New Hampshire [15]

COLORS

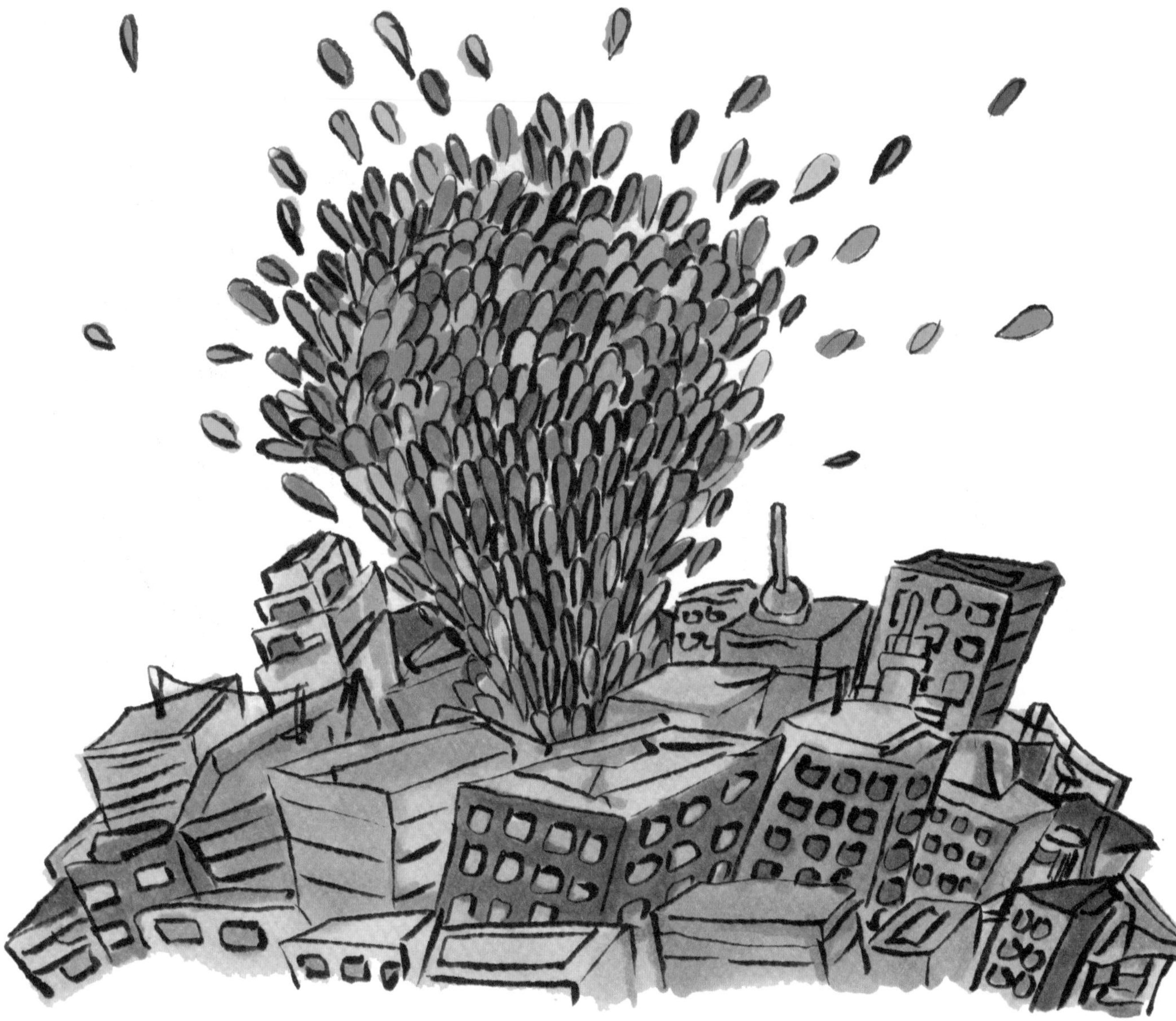

There's a store that sells colors
that've never been made
beautiful colors
in beautiful shades
of reddish gold-yellow
and pinkish blue-green
and silverish purplish aquamarine.

There's a store that sells colors
you can buy them by dozens
and give them as gifts
to your colorful cousins.
You can claim them
and name them
and pass them around
take them and paint them
all over the town.

There's a store that sells colors
quite hidden away
behind the millions of stores
that only sell gray.

THE MONSTER

The monster lived a million miles
from where my house was built
and first I ever heard of him
they said he should be kill't.

They said he's got these evil eyes
and long and pointy claws
his breath you truly would despise
when he opens up his jaws
to gobble children
far and wide.
He roams the darkened streets
and there's nowhere you can
    run and hide
when he's looking for some eats.

"He's a beast!
He can't be reasoned with,
he'd slice apart our hearts.
He's a monster through and through
and we don't want him in these parts!"

And every time
they told his tale
I grew a little more scared
and the monster got more
    teeth and claws
and he grew a little more hair.

So I live in fear today
of a monster I'll never see
and somewhere a million
    miles away
there's a monster afraid of me.

SLUMBER

You won't know all the answers
you won't get everything right
but once you learn you don't have to know 'em
you'll sleep the best at night.

The teeny-tiny giant
was only ten feet tall
and while that's giant size to you and me
to giants it's quite small.

THE
TEENY-
TINY
GIANT

Xavier Xing Xu
was terribly blue
that the number of
X-fronted words was so few.

"All the words," he would say,
"begin with an A,
or with B or with C
or even with J

or with F
or with M
or with L
or with K.
But do words ever start
    with an X?
No. No way.
Besides *xylophone*, *x-ray*,
    and the *xiphias* fish

and the Xerox machine
and your long X-mas list
there aren't many words
you can draw
or can sing
that start with an X,"
    said Xavier Xing.

But Xavier Xing Xu knew
he wasn't alone,
so he picked up the phone
and called Xelly Xang Xone,
and Xelly Xang Xone told
Xed Xingle-Xart, of the
    Xingle-Xart brothers,
who were terribly smart,
so they hatched up a plan
that would make it an art
to change all the S words
and put X at the start,
so that *start* became *xtart*
and *sing* became *xing*.

It may really xound xilly to do
    xuch a thing
but for them it was xuper
to have xo many xounds
xo many X words just
    xwimming around
like a xhark in the xea
or a xail on a xhip

or to xtand on the xhore with
with a xtone you could xkip.
It was xtupendous —
the X words abounded
with everyone xaying
they loved how it xounded.

Yes, everyone loved it,
no one minded one bit,
except Sarah Sue Simmons
and Sam Sullivan Smith.

Today you should ride in a helicopter

today you should tame a whale

today you should race

up to outer space

or at least

you should try

and fail.

Listen close to what I say
because some of it is wrong
and I need you to remind me
next time we don't get along
like when I'm mad
or when I'm sad
or when I'm not so strong.
Listen close and sing to me
this perfect little song:

"You're a special person
and I know how you feel
all the pressure's got you hurtin'
well, it's really no big deal.
What matters most
is there's birds in the trees
and bees on the flowers
and there's fish in the sea
and there's sun shining down
from a sky
that's so blue
and there's me
standing here
saying I love you."

FREEDOM

When you carve your name in the side of a tree
think of all the things it could ever be:
a house
or a fort
or a raft on the sea
that's saving a man
by setting him free.

NEW START

He didn't know
how to end anything,
only how to begin.
He started a game
then quit in the middle;
he never learned how to win.

He didn't know how to finish a laugh
or a knock-knock joke
or to finish a bath.
He never finished a book
or a meal in his life
until the day that he met his wife
and he knew he loved her
deep down in his heart
because she knew how to finish
but not how to start.

LIFE IN A CAVE

The bear cleaned his cave
ten times today
and ten times the day before.
He'll clean it again ten times tomorrow
and on Friday ten times more.
But no matter how many times he cleans
one thing stays the same
the view from the window
of his cave never seems to change.

ENEMIES

Your enemies like drawing pictures
just the same as you
they like music
and dancing
and singing and laughing
and playing a red kazoo.
And they even like
to ride on a bike
but you'll only find out when
your enemies aren't your enemies
'cause you call your enemies friends.

THE BREAKS

I broke my leg on accident;
I don't know how it happened.
I was just walking
and all of the sudden
my leg bone started snappin'.

"That sounds strange.
Are you telling the truth?"

Yes, I was just walking
then I jumped off a roof
and onto a bike
and down a ramp
with a triple flip
while holding a lamp
on top of my head
and juggling swords

with my hands tied together
by extension cords,
blindfolded twice
and wrapped in a muzzle,
singing a song
and doing a puzzle,
wearing a cape
and one red shoe,
but I don't think that has much to do
with how I broke my leg . . .
do you?

REAL LIVE DRAGON

I found a real live dragon
but I wouldn't let anyone see him
'cause my mom and my dad would probably get mad
and put him in a museum

and my teacher would say, "That dragon's cursed!"
and my friends would be overzealous,
and my sister would say she found him first,
and my brother would probably be jealous.

So I put my dragon back where I found him
'cause I realized I just couldn't bear it.
What good is having a real live dragon
if there's no one else
there to share it?

GIVE
ME
A
TRY

A magic rope
hung from the sky
with a sign that read
"Give me a try."
Should I climb it?
What if I die . . . ?
Or what if I
just walk on by?

RAINBOW

She made a rainbow out of thread
and hung it up above her bed
and she found inside the blanket fold
a little threaded pot of gold.

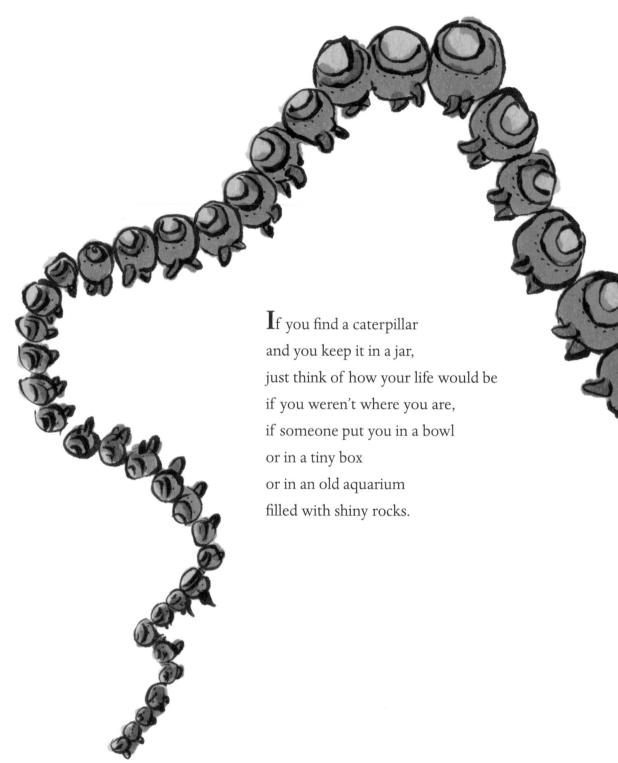

If you find a caterpillar
and you keep it in a jar,
just think of how your life would be
if you weren't where you are,
if someone put you in a bowl
or in a tiny box
or in an old aquarium
filled with shiny rocks.

BUTTERFLY

MY BIKE

I'm riding my bike
with my head in the air
through a town without hope
that's weighed down with despair.
I'm riding my bike
and mile after mile
I'm passing sad faces
and I wave
and I smile
at all of the folks
in the city of doom.
I say, "Hop on the back
of my bike
if you'd like . . .
I've got room."

Be nice to your friends
'cause you never know
when you'll be stuck
in ten feet of snow
with nowhere to stay
and nowhere to go
and no one around
but your old pal Mo,
who owns a plow
and loves you so,
and he'll wrap you up
and carry you home
and make you a fire
to warm your bones.

Be nice to your friends
'cause you never know.

I made a mistake when I wrote this
then I covered it up with some ink
then my hands got mistaken and made a mistake
and they spilled it all over the sink
so I asked for a rag to help fix it
but they brought me a rug by mistake.
Now the sink and the rug are all covered in ink
and the writing has taken a break.
Now I'm down on my knees
and a scrubbin' it clean
but the mistake that I made just keeps growin'
and I think
if I had it to do over again,
I'd've made my mistake and kept goin'.

He was mad at the stone
so he took it and threw it
as hard as he could
and cried "Why'd you do it?
You dumb stone,
it's your fault
that I tripped and I fell
and spilled all my toys
and my books down the well
and I tore up my shirt
and my right knee got hurt
and my new purple shoes
got all covered in dirt.
What were you doing there?
Dumb stone on the ground,
blocking my way
while I'm walking around!"

He was mad at the stone
so he took it and threw it
up high in the sky
and before he knew it
the stone came back down
with a crash on his head
and it knocked him right over
and it left his face red
and he laid on his back
and he yelled at the sky
for not catching the stone
when he threw it so high.

GREAT
IDEAS

A bad idea is one that starts:
"Oh, that looks so easy.
I could do that, so I will—that will be so breezy."
A good idea is one that starts
by saying "That looks fun
and it doesn't matter how hard it is—
I'd love to get it done."

BRUCE THE MOOSE

Bruce the moose
drove a caboose
and was going out of his mind
'cause instead of seeing the whole world from the front
he always just saw the behind.

BIRTHDAY!

Happy Happy Birthday
was the greatest song I knew.
Didn't matter how I sung it
sung it red or sung it blue
sung it up or down
or inside out
I always sung it true.
Happy Birthday was the greatest song,
'cause I was singing it to you.

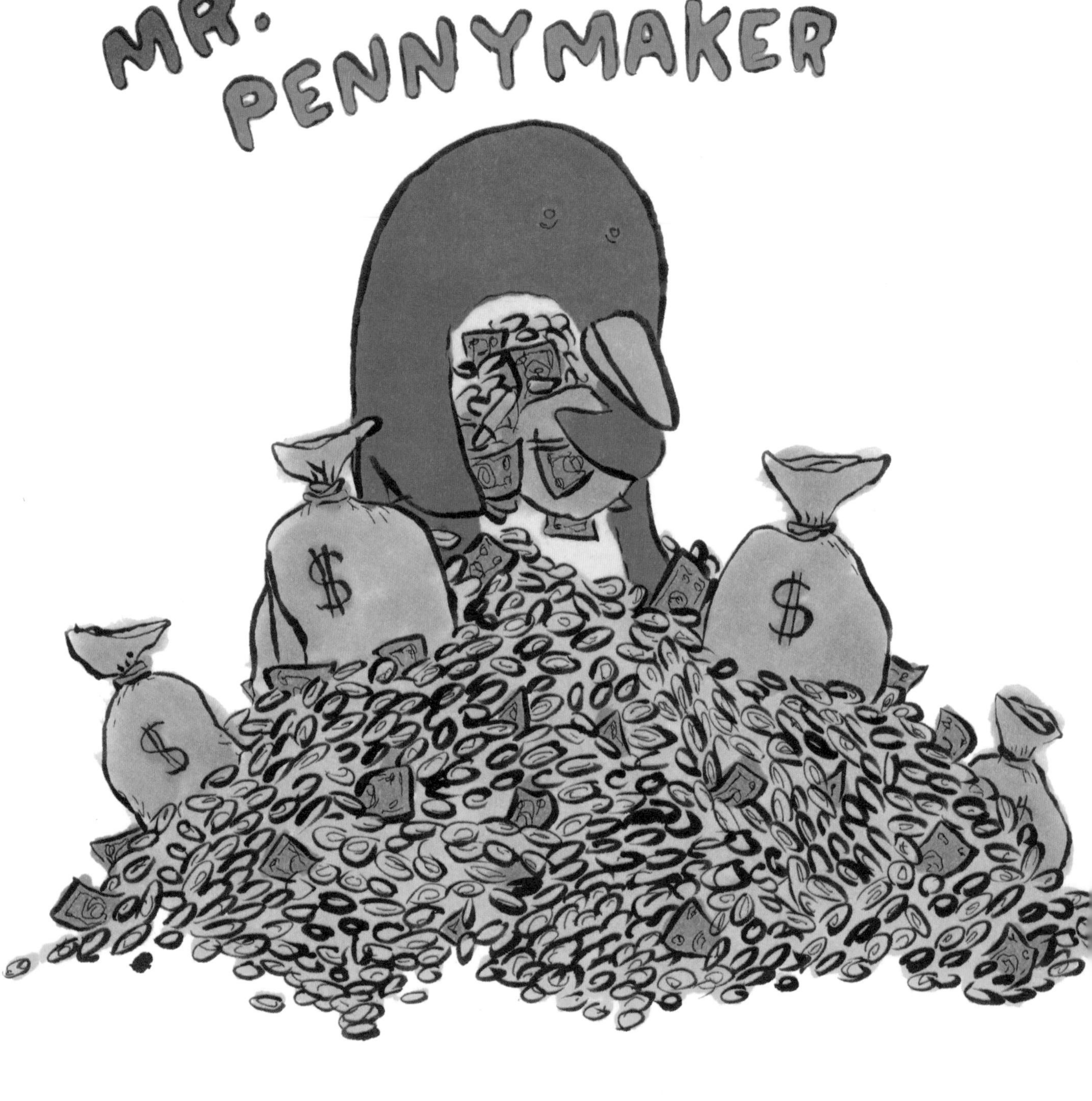
MR. PENNYMAKER

Mr. Pennymaker
was a very wealthy guy
he bought anything and everything
you'd ever want to buy.

He bought tigers, houses, cars, and mountains,
lakes and trees and oceans
he bought jewels the size of butterflies
he even bought emotions.

He'd buy and spend
till in the end, he bought up outer space,
then he sailed off on a rocket screaming,
"I own every place!"

But when he got to space
he found
all the money he'd ever spent
had gotten him only
sad and lonely
and it wasn't worth a cent.

TRAVEL STORIES

Her quiet stories were best of all
'cause she never wrote 'em down
she lived 'em out by travelin'
and roamin' town to town
meetin' folks
and sharin' jokes
as the world went round and round. . . .

Someday you'll get bigger
bigger than today
and you might be the president
or the star of the high-school play.
Someday you'll be bigger
bigger than you think.
But remember:
no matter how big you get
you still used to bathe
in a sink.

QUIET JOE

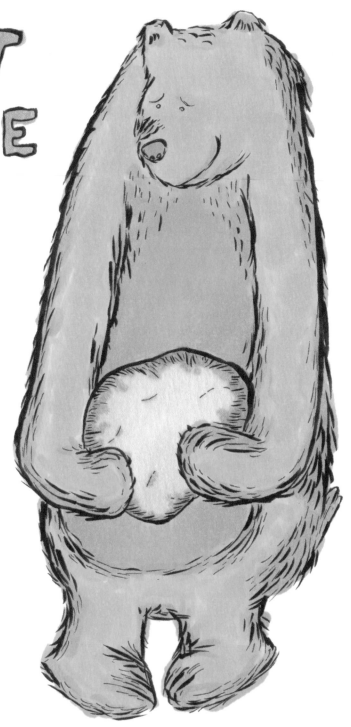

"There's a rock in the road!"
said Timmy Toad.
"How will we get around?"

"A rock in the road!"
Aunt Mimmy moaned.
"But I have to get to town."

"A rock in the road!"
cried Sally Sue.
"Let's blame whoever did it."

"A rock in the road, that's ballyhoo.
Let's take a picture with it."
And down the line they all exclaimed,
"That Rock!" "That Rock!"
Each one complained;
they howled
and yelled
and whined
and screamed
and cried.
They sat like that
for an hour or so
when from the end of the line
walked Quiet Joe
soft
and sweet
and small
and slow in stride.

He looked at everyone
yapping and fussing,
hooting and honking and
snapping and cussing,
and with a heave and a ho
Joe moved that rock aside.

And they all stood looking
as he walked round
past the rock
and into town
to the ice-cream shop,
where he sat down
and ordered
himself a heaping
slice of pie.

So if you find yourself
behind a rock
stuck in the muck
and starting to squawk
like everyone else
on down the block,
just keep one thought in mind.
Sometimes it only takes one man
to move one thing
with his own two hands
for everyone in town
to get on by.

ROBOTS

Whenever you build a robot
make sure to give him a switch
that changes him from bad to good
and remember which is which.

The world might be ending tomorrow

or maybe another day soon

or maybe six Tuesdays from this coming Wednesday

or maybe the twelfth day in June.

The world might end

I've been told by some people

or maybe it'll just keep on going

the world might end

but I'm telling you, friend

let's live

like there's no way of knowing. . . .

LIFE

WISHERS

Make a wish on an eyelash
make a wish on a cake
make a wish on a penny
make a wish on a snake
make a wish on a blade of grass
make a wish on a hug
make a wish on a crocodile
make a wish on a bug
make a wish on a wish
on a star, on the moon,
on a picture of a baby cat
riding a balloon.
Make a wish on anything,
make one or two or three,
and maybe if you get your wish,
you could make a wish for me.

The shark without teeth
is the friendliest beast
to ever have swum
the Great Barrier Reef.
So if ever you meet,
he'll surely be sweet
but I can't say the same
for his big brother Keith.

THE SHARK WITHOUT TEETH

Dilly and Dally

started a band

with Billy and Sally

and Agnes and Graham.

"We'll make wonderful music,

find fortune and fame.

No one that hears it

will ever complain

and all that we need is a fantastic name."

So Dilly spoke up and he said,

"Dilly's Band!"

And Dally said, "That name just sounds silly, man.

We'll call it Dally's All-Star Cast."

And Billy laughed, and Sally passed.

And Billy said, "Let's call it Billy's Explosion,"

and Agnes said, "I bet that name has been chosen."

So Sally said, "Sally and the Wonderful Weasels,"

and Agnes said, "Agnes and the Artistic Easels,"

and Graham said, "You all are just being insane.

Let's choose a name that's just simple and plain.

How 'bout Graham? That's a name that'll stick in your brain."

And then Agnes got angry,
and Dally got sad
and Billy got bored
and Sally got mad.
And everyone argued
for so terribly long
that the band had to break up
before they wrote their first song.

THE BAND

SUNSHINE

She blew a kiss
it missed my face
and drifted into outer space
and kissed the sun
and made it smile
now it's been bright
for quite a while.

Today I met a wizard
who sold me a wooden stick.
He told me it was magic
and could do all kinds of tricks.
If I held the stick and practiced my swing,
I could get better at ball.
If I used the stick when I climbed a hill,
it would help me if I fall.
If I tied some bristles to the stick,
I could turn it into a broom,
then I could come to the wizard's house
and sweep his living room. . . .

THE WIZARD

WAKE UP YOUR BRAIN!

Kick a ball in a hoop,
put a cone on a scoop,
take a dip in the sand,
eat a handful of soup.

Change up your game
and wake up your brain,
take your dog on a wonderful jog in the rain.
And remember when you go to bed
keep your head at the foot
and your feet at the head.

THE UNICORN GLADE

The unicorns played
in the unicorn glade
where the unicorn tree
cast uniform shade
on the saltwater pond
and they jumped off the rocks
and had cannonball contests
and wonderful talks
about clouds
and a thousand more summertime things—
it's astounding the ideas that summertime brings
like who would do what
and what would get made,
when they had to grow up
would their memories fade?
And they'd talk and they'd swim
and they'd laugh through the night.
in the unicorn glade
where the future was bright.

BOX CAT

Silly cat,
why don't you go
and see the world?
You're free, you know.
There's so much out there
yet you lay
in a box
in the yard
and sleep all day.

I lay in a box,
this much is true.
But who is sillier,
me or you?

That world out there is your world too.
And while I lounge about all day,
you sit inside
and you watch me lay.

SING A SONG

Don't forget to sing today
in a funny voice in a funny way,
to dance around
all by yourself
or shout out loud
with someone else,
a song with guitar
or a song with drums
or a song you whistle
or a song you hum.

Don't forget to sing today
in your special voice
in your special way.

Because there might come a time
some years from now
where you need to sing
but won't know how.

So just to be safe
you should do it today
and tomorrow
and the next
and on all the way
till you're big and you're grown
and it's so unexpected
for an adult to be singing
because life is too hectic
and adults are all calm
and reserved and collected.

Keep singing for them
because they want to sing too
but they've all forgotten
so it's all up to you.

NONE

Take what you need
just enough for yourself
otherwise you're taking from someone else.
And how much fun
can it really be
when they've got none
and you've got three?

THE WHOLE WIDE WORLD

When you live in a world of dirt
it's easy to get all dirty
when you live in a world of hurt
it's easy to get all hurty
when you live in a world of fun
it's easy to find things funny
when you live in a world of sun
it's easy to find things sunny.

But when you live in a world
that's full of dirt and full of sun
    and full of hurt
and full of fun and full of worse,
it's easy to get confused and curse,
it's easy to get all runny

to run away
and hide in a box
and cover it up with sticks
    and rocks
and never come out
and never make friends
and never go sailing
and never pretend.

When you live in a world
with so many things,
it's easy to see all the trouble
    it brings
but when it hurts
remember the sun
and when there's dirt
remember the fun
and when it's worse
remember the ones
who need your help
'cause they're stuck too

and maybe together you'll
    make it through
and you'll find a place
where it's always sunny
and you tell your jokes and
    they're always funny
and the dirt and hurt and worse
are gone
and a big bright future
rolls on and on.

MAKE MAGIC

DO GOOD

Make magic

do good.

Be who you are.

Be what you should.

See what you can.

Live like you could.

Take a stand.

Get understood.

Make magic

do good.

Share secrets.

Start starts.

Build brains.

Hold hands.

Break chains.

Heart hearts.

Make magic

do good.

Be honest.

Be better.

Make magic

do good

now and forever.

My name is Dallas Clayton. I write books and draw pictures, and I travel the world and read stories to children of all ages and talk to them about their lives and jump into water and climb up trees and paint walls and have adventures. It's my job. I swear. It didn't used to be my job. One day I just decided that's what I wanted to do, and then it happened. Life can be pretty amazing sometimes like that. Maybe if you have a cool idea or a fun dream or something inside of you that just seems like it needs to get done, you should just try to make it real. I bet if you do, great things will happen.